This book is dedicated to
Parker and Annie Rivera.

MASCOT BOOKS

www.mascotbooks.com

A is for Atlanta

©2018 Ryan Rivera. All Rights Reserved. No part of this publication may be reproduced, stored in a retrieval system or transmitted in any form by any means electronic, mechanical, or photocopying, recording or otherwise without the permission of the author.

For more information, please contact:
Mascot Books
620 Herndon Parkway #320
Herndon, VA 20170
info@mascotbooks.com

Library of Congress Control Number: 2017908407

CPSIA Code: PRT0618A
ISBN-13: 978-1-63177-860-5

Printed in the United States

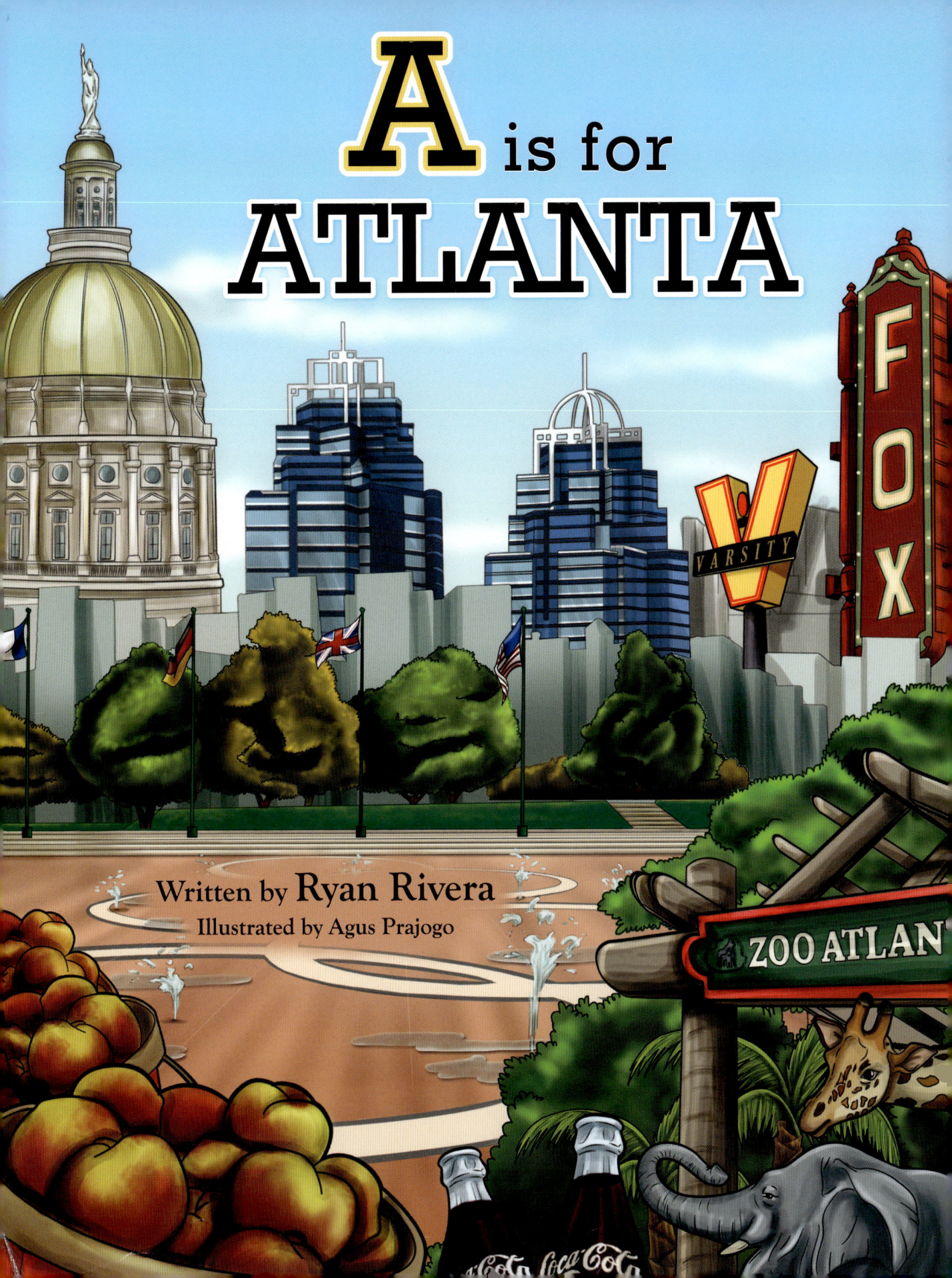

A is for ATLANTA

Written by Ryan Rivera

Illustrated by Agus Prajogo

A is for Atlanta,
the city we know and love.
This beautiful place in Georgia
is a special gift from up above.

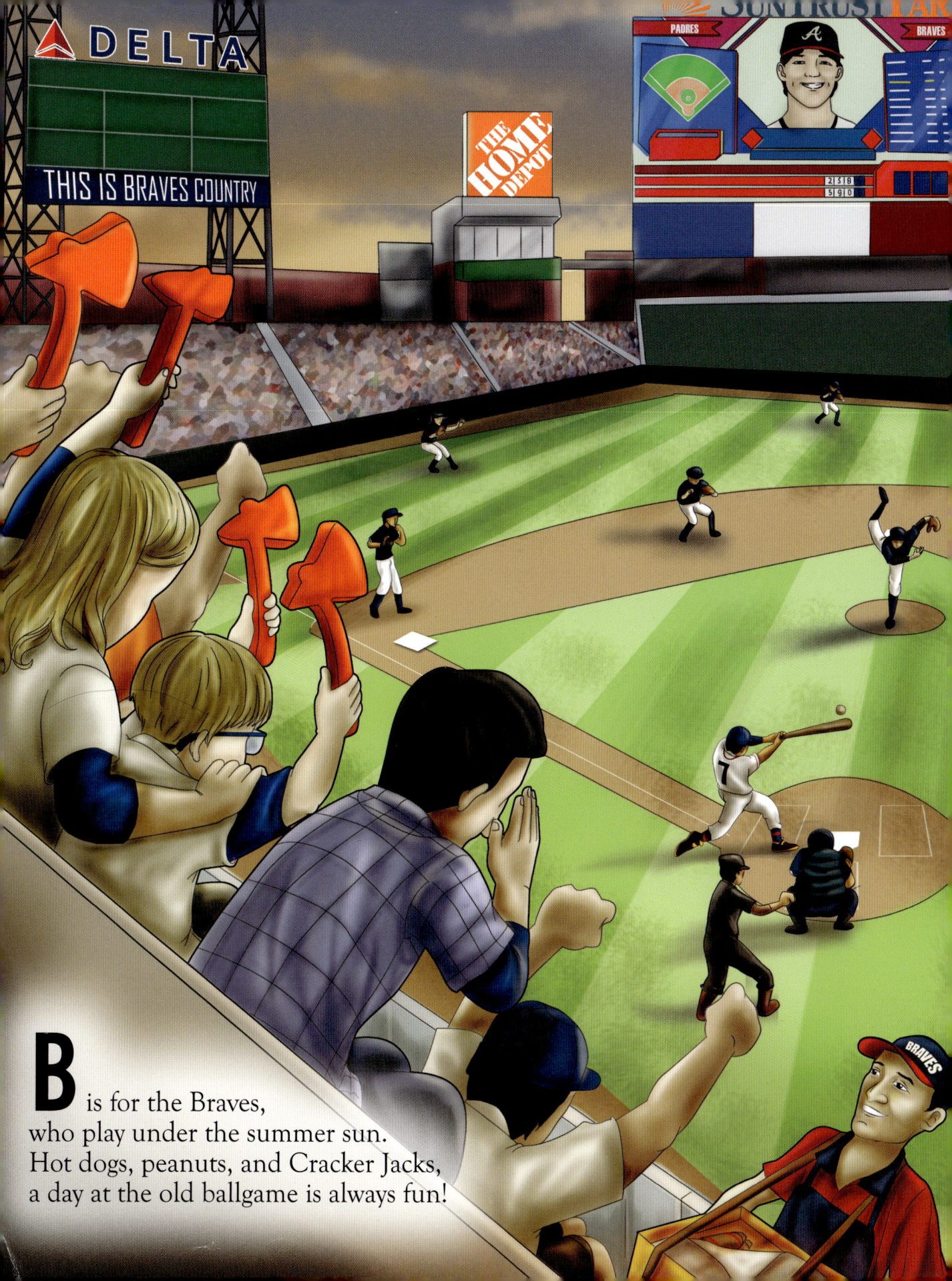

B is for the Braves,
who play under the summer sun.
Hot dogs, peanuts, and Cracker Jacks,
a day at the old ballgame is always fun!

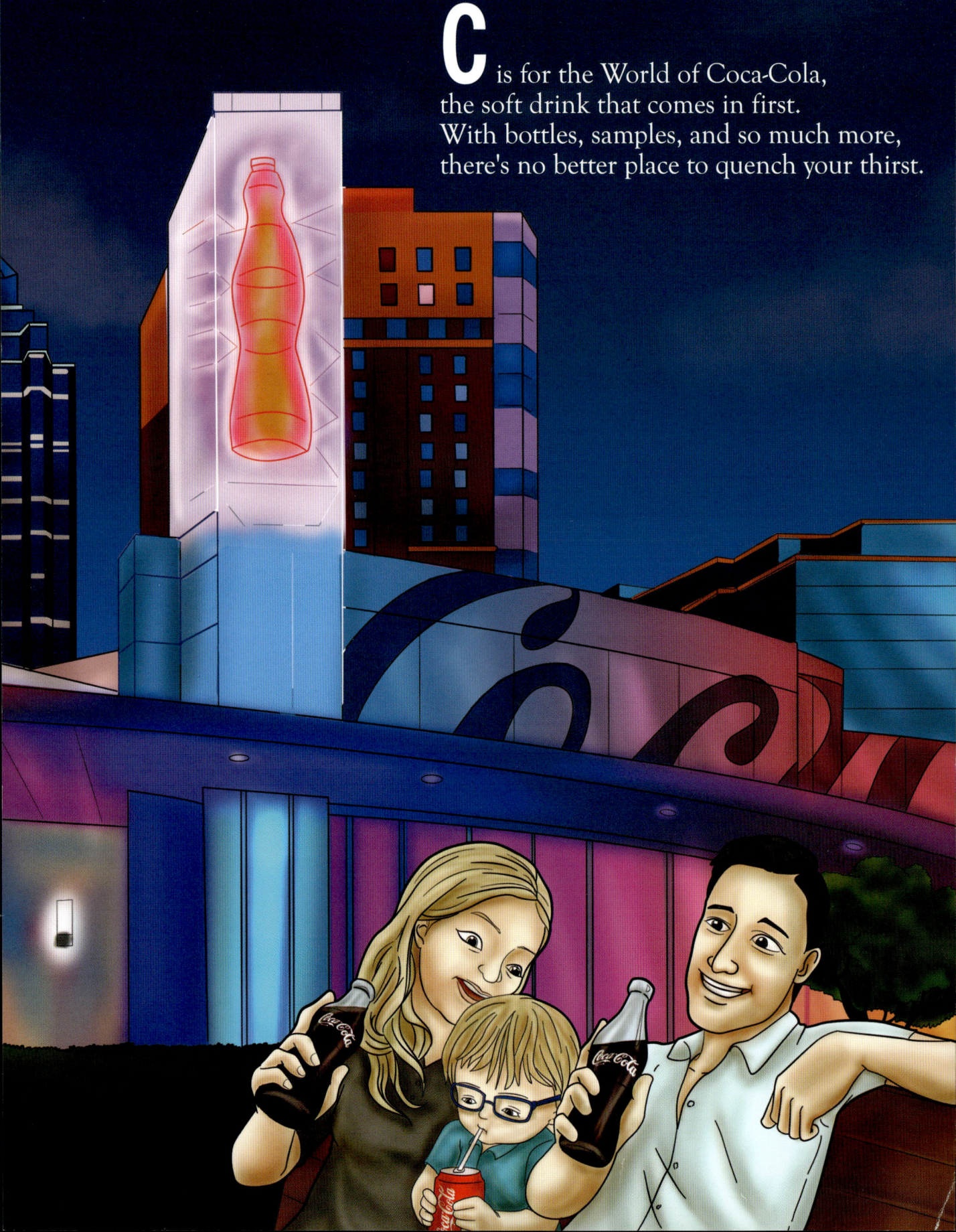

C is for the World of Coca-Cola,
the soft drink that comes in first.
With bottles, samples, and so much more,
there's no better place to quench your thirst.

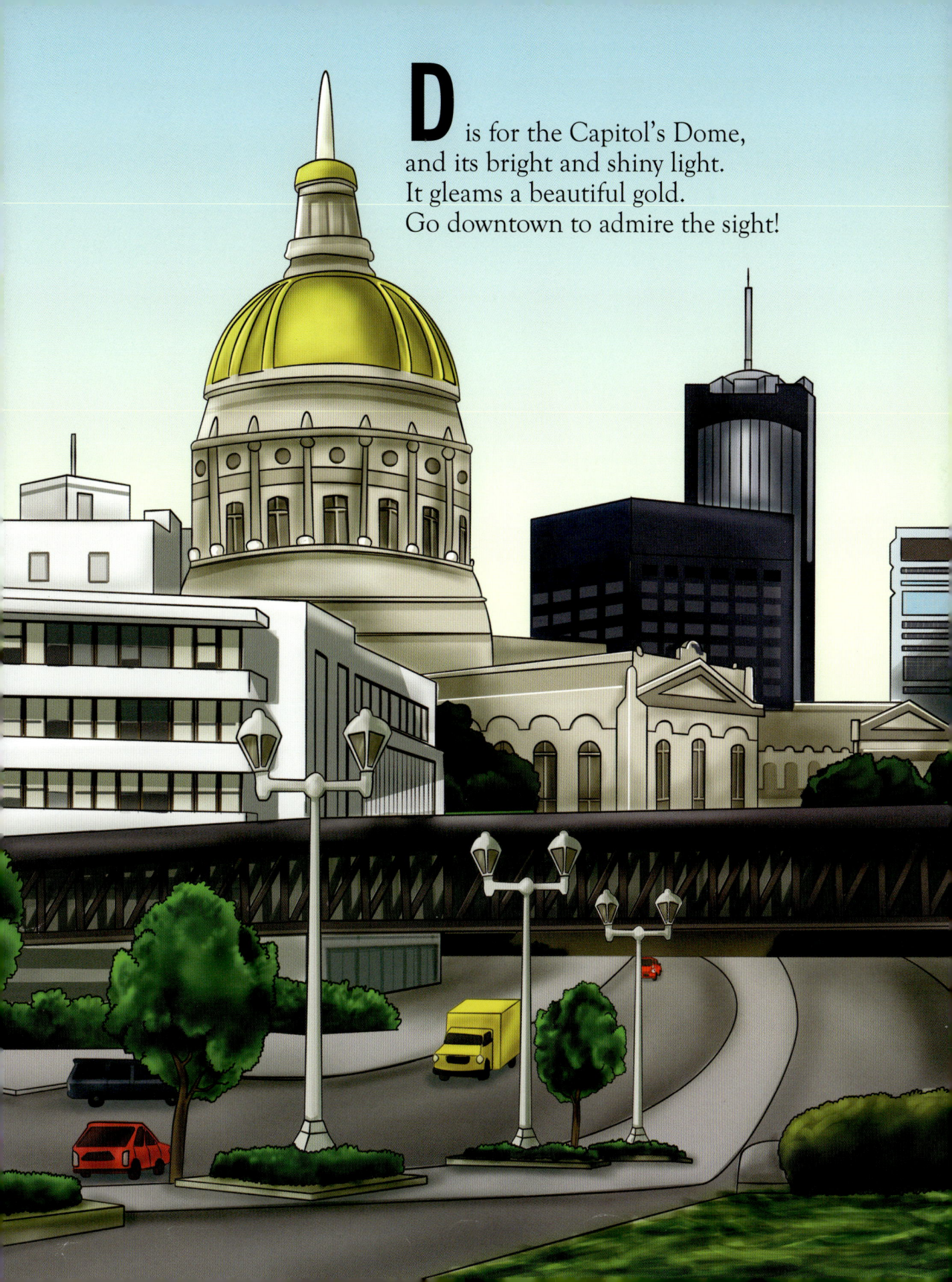

D is for the Capitol's Dome,
and its bright and shiny light.
It gleams a beautiful gold.
Go downtown to admire the sight!

E is for Elephants at the Atlanta Zoo.
They roam and play beyond the front gate.
With lions, giraffes, zebras, and more,
you'll need to arrive early and stay late.

F is for the Atlanta Falcons,
the football team we admire and adore.
Win or lose, we count on Freddie the Falcon
to be there until the Falcons' final score!

G is for the Georgia Aquarium, home to many colorful fish. With whales, dolphins, and penguins, it's a place you don't want to miss!

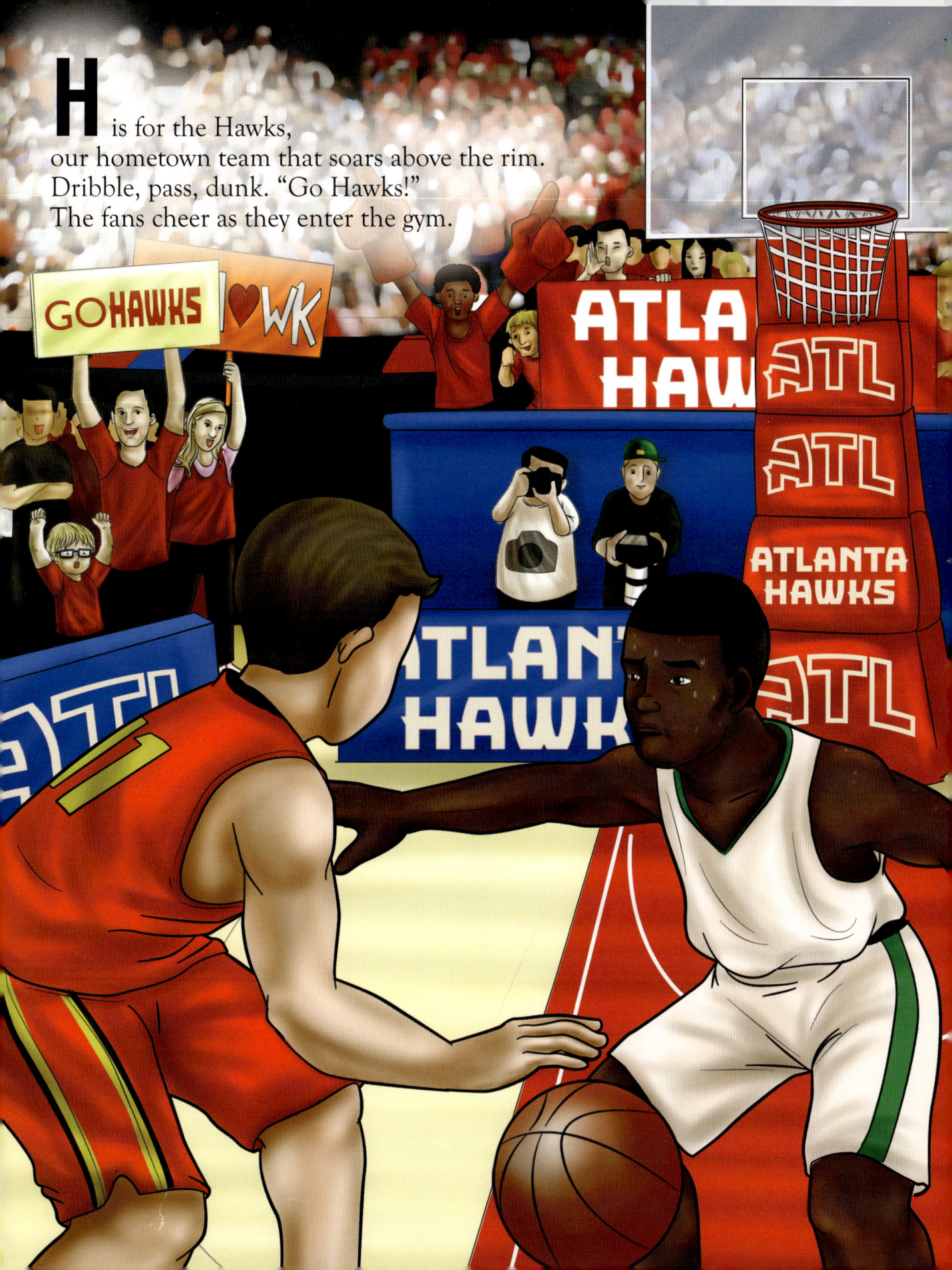

H is for the Hawks,
our hometown team that soars above the rim.
Dribble, pass, dunk. "Go Hawks!"
The fans cheer as they enter the gym.

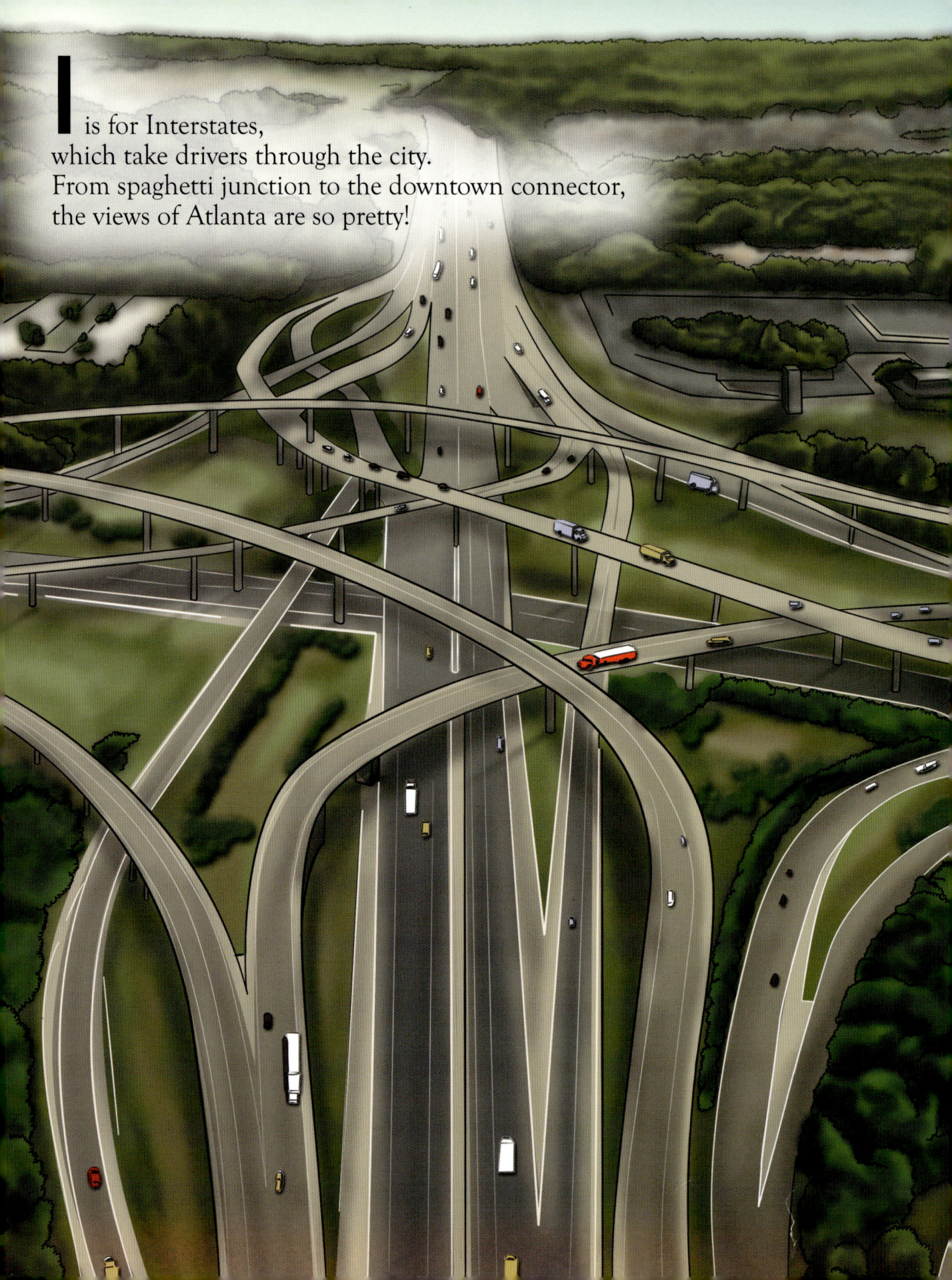

I is for Interstates,
which take drivers through the city.
From spaghetti junction to the downtown connector,
the views of Atlanta are so pretty!

J is for Hartsfield-Jackson Airport, where airplanes come and go all day. Some people visit Atlanta to explore, but some call it home and stay.

K is for Martin Luther King, Jr.,
Atlanta's most important son.
We thank him for freedom and equality,
and the many victories he won.

L is for Locomotives,
which go *Choo Choo* across the town!
MARTA, Amtrak, and freight trains,
leave the station with the throttle down!

M is for Stone Mountain,
our famous rock and Atlanta landmark.
We can take the cable car or hike to the top,
for a beautiful view before dark!

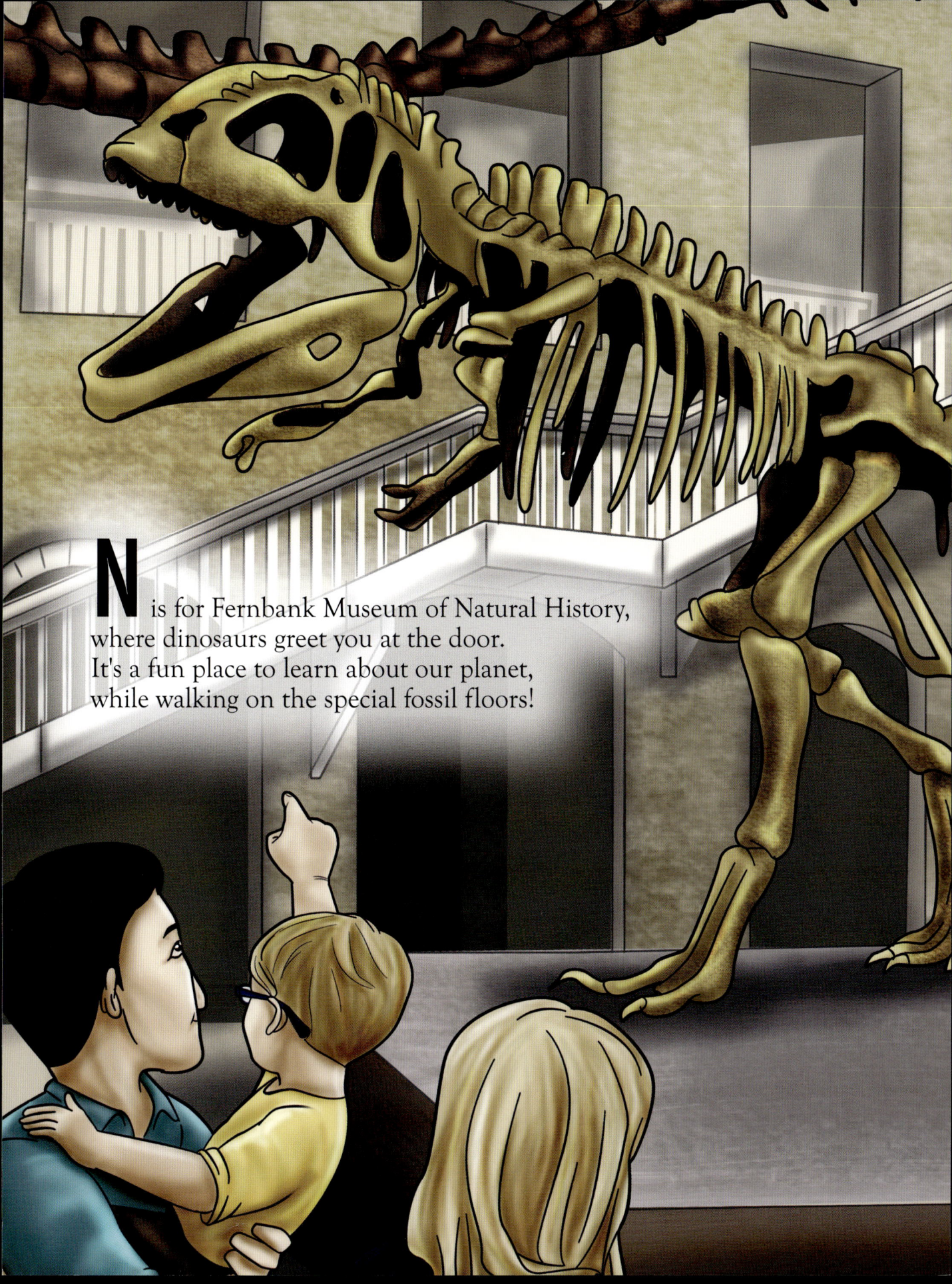

N is for Fernbank Museum of Natural History, where dinosaurs greet you at the door.
It's a fun place to learn about our planet, while walking on the special fossil floors!

O is for Centennial Olympic Park, and its fountain with each Olympic ring. It's a favorite spot for kids of all ages, to play, run, laugh, and sing!

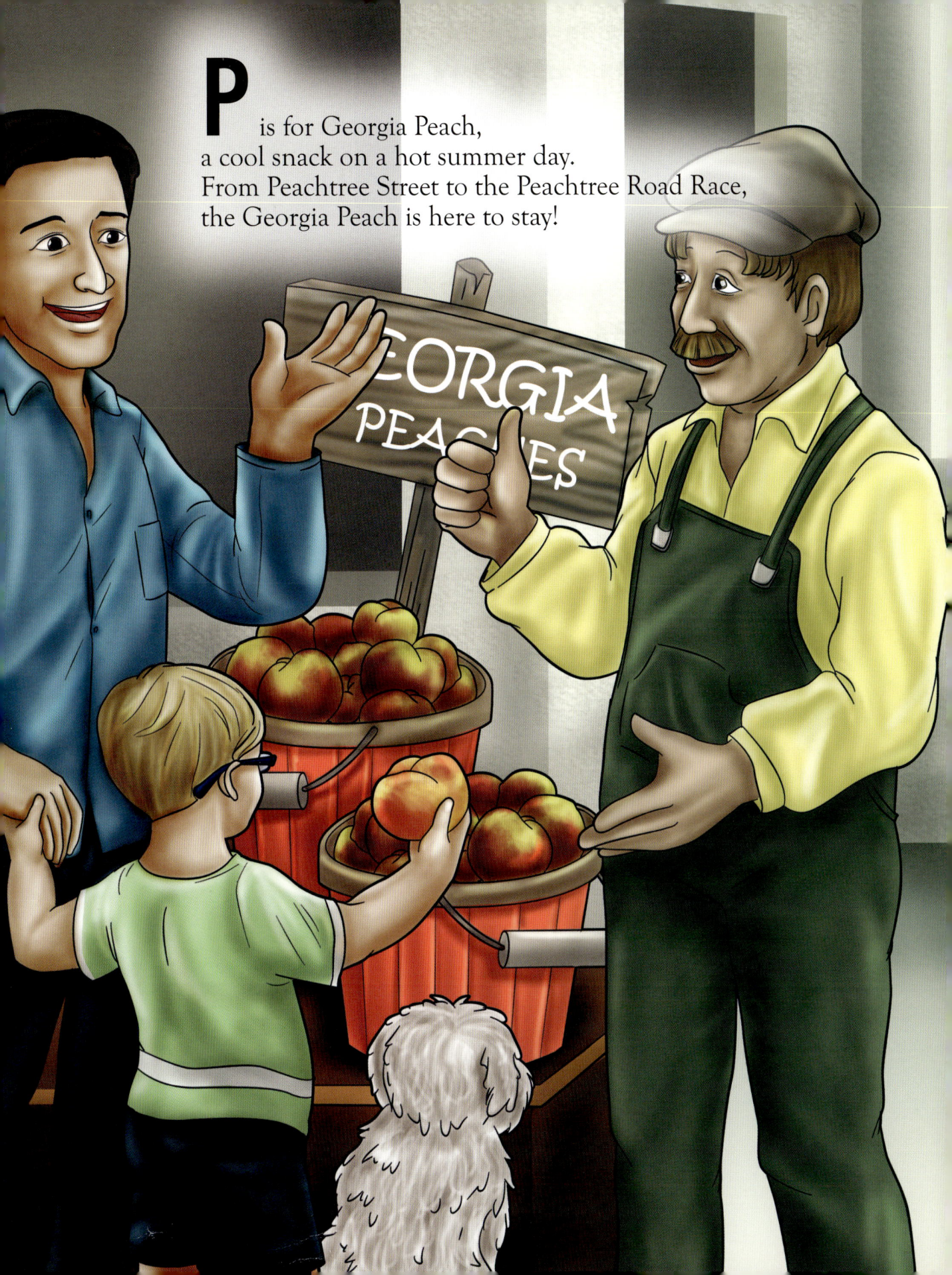

P is for Georgia Peach,
a cool snack on a hot summer day.
From Peachtree Street to the Peachtree Road Race,
the Georgia Peach is here to stay!

Q is for the Quacking Ducks that walk along the Piedmont Park shore. With peaceful sounds and scenic views, it's a special place you're sure to adore.

R is for the Chattahoochee River, a favorite spot to hike, fish, and raft. In the cool breeze, tree leaves shiver while we enjoy games, arts, and crafts!

S is for Skyscrapers,
which stand so tall in the sky.
Look up to admire the buildings,
and watch the birds and planes fly by!

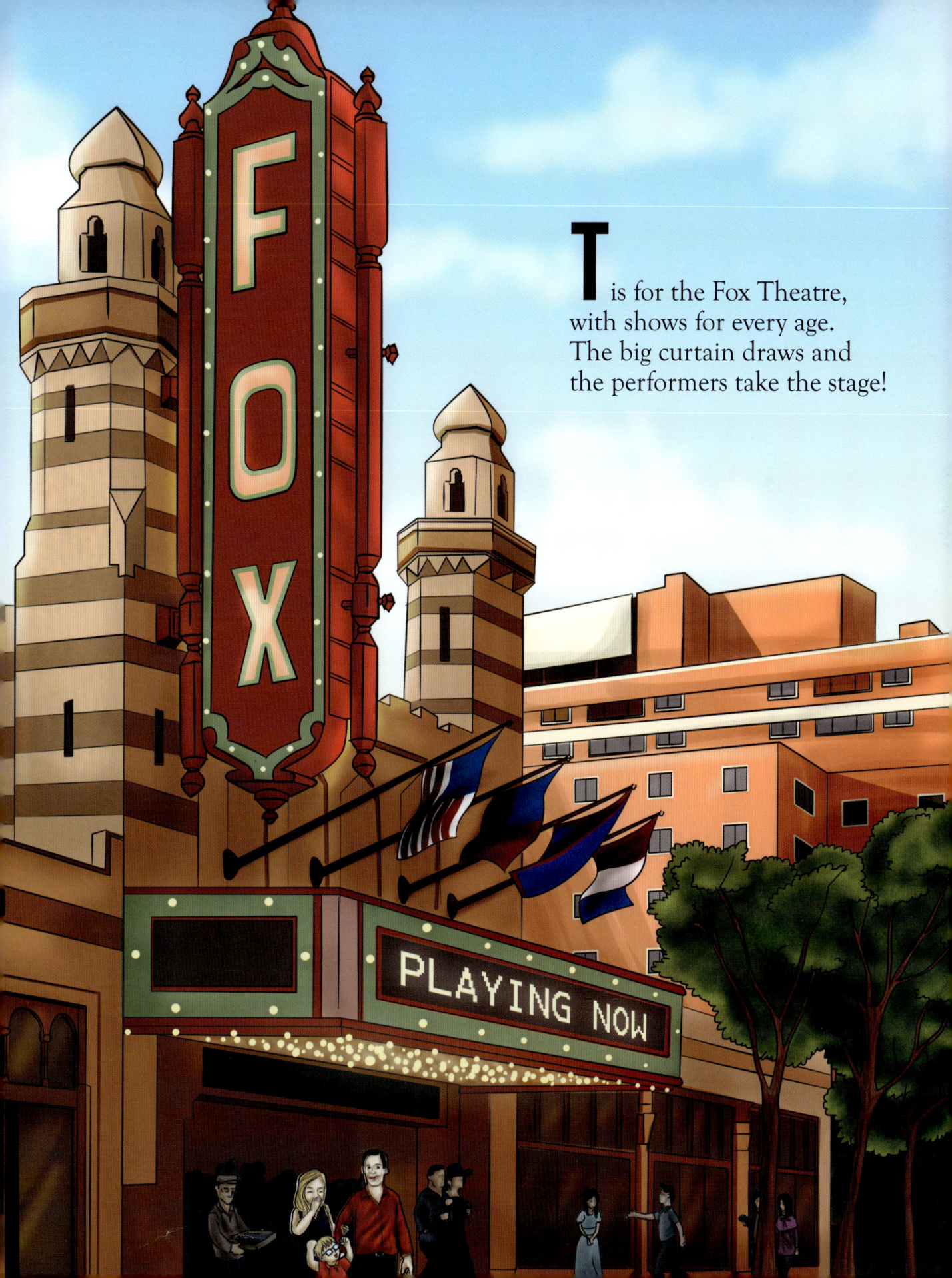

T is for the Fox Theatre, with shows for every age. The big curtain draws and the performers take the stage!

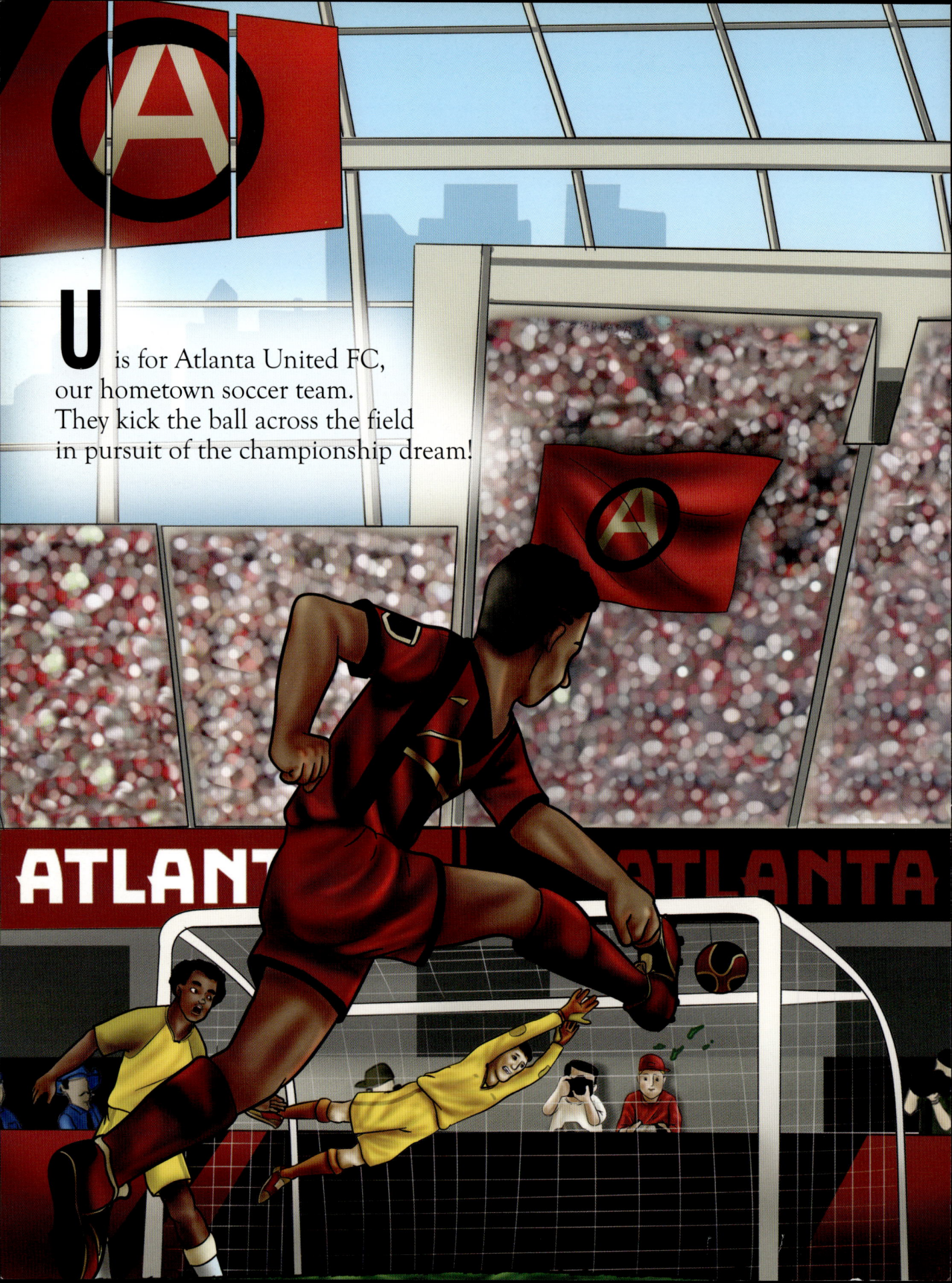

U is for Atlanta United FC, our hometown soccer team. They kick the ball across the field in pursuit of the championship dream!

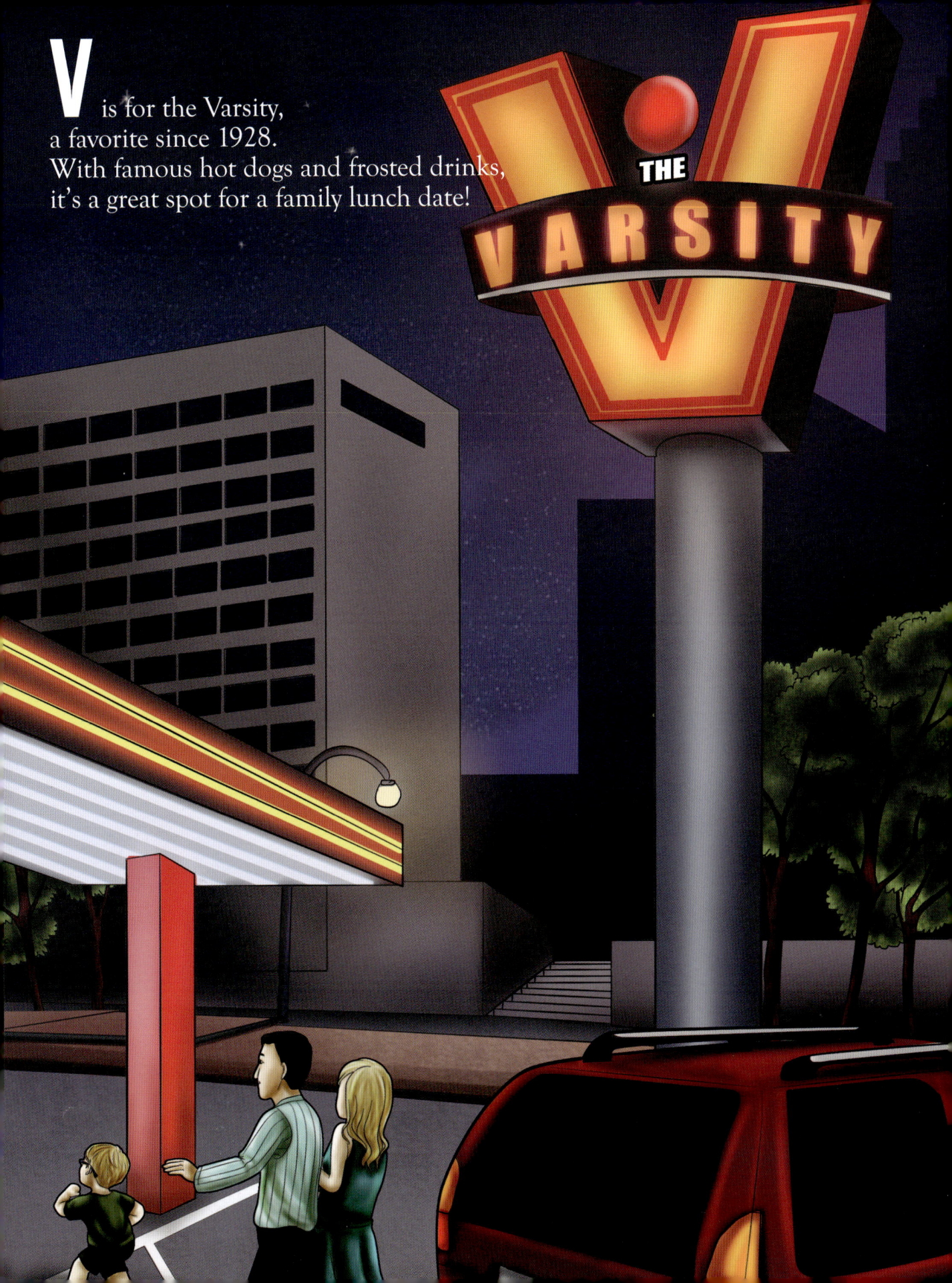

V is for the Varsity,
a favorite since 1928.
With famous hot dogs and frosted drinks,
it's a great spot for a family lunch date!

W is for West Paces Ferry,
where the governor's mansion stands tall.
From south of Vinings to the heart of Buckhead,
the views from this road are beautiful in the fall!

X is for Exit 249C,
which says downtown attractions this way!
When we exit and head toward downtown,
we know it'll be a special day!

Y is for you,
my little Atlanta fan!
If you want to see our city's beautiful views,
just say so and we'll load up the van!

Z is for zzzz.
Sweet dreams and sleep tight!
Goodnight, my little Georgia Peach,
and dream of Atlanta through the night.

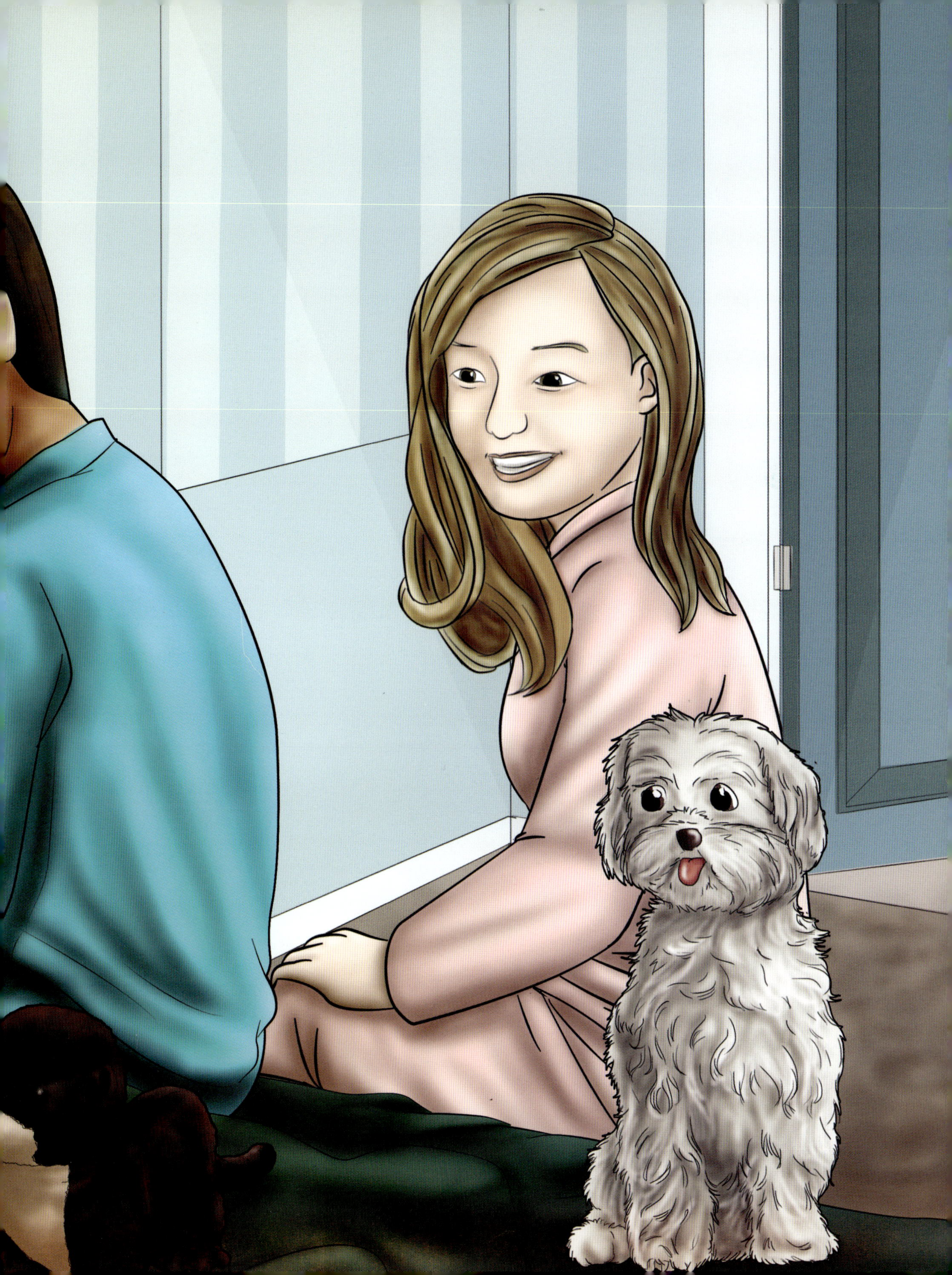

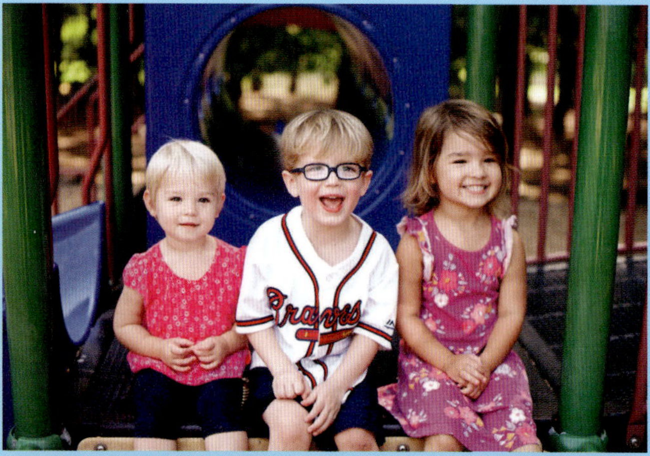

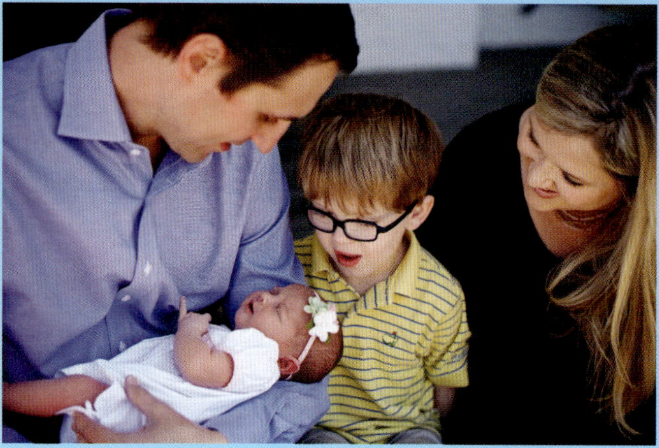

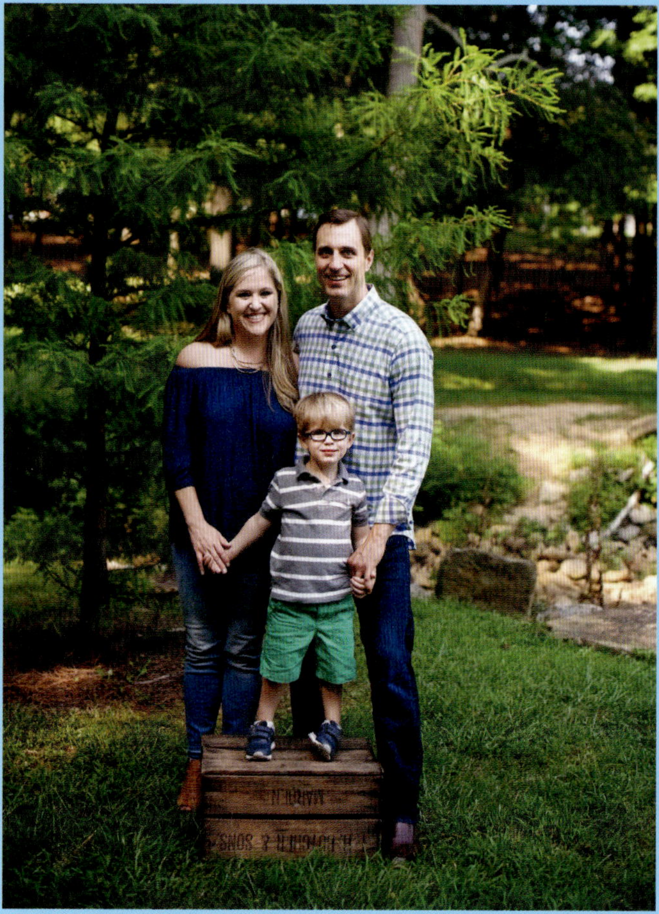

About the Author

Originally from Springfield, Illinois, Ryan Rivera has called Atlanta home since his graduation from the University of Iowa in 2001. He lives in Smyrna with his wife, Casey, and their children, Parker and Annie. Ryan and his family enjoy spending time at SunTrust Park, Zoo Atlanta, and the Georgia Aquarium. When not visiting one of Atlanta's many great attractions, they enjoy spending time in Marietta with Parker and Annie's cousins, Lauren and Reese Rivera, and with family in Valley, Alabama.

MASCOT
BOOKS

Have a book idea?
Contact us at:

info@mascotbooks.com | www.mascotbooks.com